EAT YOUR DINNER!

Virginia Miller

WALKER BOOKS

AND SUBSIDIARIES

LONDON • BOSTON • SYDNEY

George came looking
for Bartholomew with his dinner.
"Dinner's ready, Ba," he said.

"Have you washed your face and hands?"

"Nah!" said Bartholomew.

George said, "Sit up, Ba,

and eat your dinner."

"Nah, nah, nah, nah,

NAH!" said Bartholomew.

"Eat your

George said in a big voice.

Bartholomew ate one spoonful,

then he had a little rest.

George sat down at the table
and began to eat his dinner.

Bartholomew watched
until George had finished.

Then George left the table
and returned with a large honey cake.

He cut a slice and ate it and when
he had finished he took the rest away.

Suddenly Bartholomew thought,
Eat your dinner!

He thought of the honey cake…

with the pretty pink icing...

and the cherry on top...

and he licked his bowl perfectly clean.

He went to find George.

"Have you finished, Ba?" George asked.
"Nah," said Bartholomew, and George smiled
and gave him the slice of cake
with the cherry on top.